Rosie and Sarah ran toward the sound of the clanging fire engine bells. As they turned the corner, three large white horses pulling a red fire wagon with hoses thundered past them. Followed by another. And another one loaded with ladders.

"Must be a big fire," said Sarah.

People were running down the street after the wagons. Rosie and Sarah stopped an old woman with a kerchief on her head, still wearing her apron.

"Have you heard?" Rosie asked her. "Where's the fire?"

"Washington Square," the woman answered.

They looked up over the buildings toward the square. In the distance, a pillar of black smoke rose into the sky.

"Freyda works there," Rosie said quietly.

FIRE!

FIRE!

THE BEGINNINGS OF THE LABOR MOVEMENT

BY BARBARA DIAMOND GOLDIN

ILLUSTRATED BY JAMES WATLING

PUFFIN BOOKS

PUFFIN BOOKS
Published by the Penguin Group
Penguin Books USA Inc., 375 Hudson Street, New York, New York 10014, U.S.A.
Penguin Books Ltd, 27 Wrights Lane, London W8 5TZ, England
Penguin Books Australia Ltd, Ringwood, Victoria, Australia
Penguin Books Canada Ltd, 10 Alcorn Avenue, Toronto, Ontario, Canada M4V 3B2
Penguin Books (N.Z.) Ltd, 182-190 Wairau Road, Auckland 10, New Zealand

Penguin Books Ltd, Registered Offices: Harmondsworth, Middlesex, England

First published in the United States of America by Viking Penguin,
a division of Penguin Books USA Inc., 1992
Published in Puffin Books, 1997

1 3 5 7 9 10 8 6 4 2

THE LIBRARY OF CONGRESS HAS CATALOGED THE VIKING EDITION AS FOLLOWS:
Goldin, Barbara Diamond.
Fire! : the beginnings of the labor movement / by Barbara Diamond Goldin :
illustrated by James Watling
p. cm. — (Once upon America)
Summary: In 1911 Rosie becomes involved in the struggle for better working
conditions in factories when fire rips through the Triangle Shirtwaist
factory, where her older sister Freyda is employed.
ISBN 0-670-84475-6
1. Triangle Shirtwaist Company—Fire, 1911—Juvenile Fiction.
[1. Triangle Shirtwaist Company—Fire, 1911—Fiction.
2. Industrial safety—Fiction.] I. Watling, James, ill.
II. Title III. Series
PZ7.G5674Fi 1992 [Fic]—dc20 91-40759 CIP AC

Puffin Books ISBN 0-14-034685-6

Printed in the United States of America

ONCE UPON AMERICA® is a registered trademark of Viking Penguin,
a division of Penguin Books USA Inc.

To Jane Yolen—favorite author, master teacher,
mentor, and dear friend.
With love and thanks.

Contents

Hurry Home, Rosie!   1

Spelling Lists and Old Bony   7

Sabbath Dinner   14

Clanging Bells   19

The Fire   25

Everything Burning   32

One More Question   39

Changes Ahead   44

About This Book   53

Hurry Home, Rosie!

Rosie waited for her best friend, Sarah, outside the school door. The March wind played with her skirt and she wished she could play, too. But no, she had to go straight home, help Max with his homework, and help Mama get ready for the Sabbath.

My sister Freyda is lucky, Rosie thought. She gets up and goes to work, earns money, goes to the movies with her friends. She's always going out. All I get to do is go to school and home, school and home.

Just then Sarah tapped her on the shoulder.

"Did Miss Callahan yell at you today?" she asked. "You look so glum."

"That grouch!" Rosie did an imitation of Miss Callahan's waddle. Sarah giggled. "That old snuffle bag was in one of her moods," Rosie continued. "She washed Izzie's mouth out with that awful yellow lye soap. Boy, will his parents be mad when they get the note."

"Poor Izzie." Sarah grinned. "He must have talked back again."

Rosie nodded, grinning too.

"Do you have a penny?" Sarah asked suddenly, changing the subject.

"No," said Rosie.

"I do. What should we buy?"

"I don't have much time," warned Rosie. "Mama wants me right home."

"Again?"

"Again," Rosie answered.

The two girls linked arms and walked quickly together down the street.

"Let's go to Orchard Street," said Rosie. She loved to see all the activity on the shopping street. The people going here and there, the horse-drawn wagons, the pushcarts with mountains of shoes and hats and pants, sweet potatoes, candy, and boots. You never knew what you would find there.

They passed the merry-go-round. Its six wooden

horses were on top of a wagon pulled by a real horse, an old and bony one. Rosie's brother, Max, talked to the horse whenever he could.

The air about her was filled with the shouts of push-cart peddlers and the *clop clop* of horseshoes on cobblestones. Children laughed and screamed, playing in the street. Rosie knew all the games. Roll the hoop, tag, tops, duck-on-a-rock. But she had no time to stop. No time to play.

"Hurry home, Rosie." Her mama's words echoed in her ears. Mama meant well. She worked so hard herself. When she wasn't cooking and cleaning, she was sewing piecework—homework, they called it. Always the sewing homework piled on the sofa. Collars to put on coats, hems and buttons, too. Papa worked hard also, painting houses. But even with Papa and Mama and Freyda working, there was never enough money.

"If only Mama would let me quit school," Rosie moaned. "Then I could go to work like Freyda. I could make money and Mama wouldn't have to do so much homework."

"But you're only eleven," Sarah said.

"There are eleven-year-old girls working in factories," Rosie told her. "Like Frances Gotlieb. She just hides in a bin when the inspector comes along."

"Your mother would never let you. You know that. You're too good a student. Now, how should we spend this penny?"

Sarah held her penny right in front of Rosie's nose. Rosie crossed her eyes looking at it, making Sarah laugh.

"Indian nuts?"

Rosie shook her head no.

"Pretzels?"

No, again.

"A pickled tomato?"

No.

"The candy store?"

Sarah was sure Rosie would say yes to this idea. But Rosie knew what she wanted. She pulled Sarah down the street until they were right in front of the fortune-teller.

The girls were a little afraid of the old lady with strange bright clothes, warts on her cheek, and a parrot on her shoulder. She played the hand organ but she didn't talk. Maybe she couldn't talk. But if you put one penny in her cup, the parrot did his trick. He would pick a slip of paper out of a box with his beak and give it to you. On it was your fortune.

"Is it a good one?" Sarah asked. She never held her hand out for the slip of paper. She didn't trust the bird.

"A different one," answered Rosie.

"Well, what is it?" asked her friend impatiently.

" 'Changes ahead,' That's all. 'Changes ahead.' "

"What does that mean?" said Sarah.

"I don't know," said Rosie. "Maybe that I'll be quitting school." She tucked the piece of paper into her skirt pocket to keep it safe.

"I don't want Mama to find it," Rosie said to Sarah. "You know what she would say. 'Wasting a penny on such garbage. Feh!' "

They continued home. When they reached the stoop in front of Rosie's building, Sarah said good-bye. Her building was down the street.

"See you tomorrow after services?" Sarah asked her friend.

"Meet me right here," said Rosie.

Spelling Lists
and
Old Bony

As Rosie opened the door to her building the smells of Sabbath cooking surrounded her. Everyone cooked ahead of time, since no food could be prepared on the Sabbath.

She climbed the stairs to the third floor. Their apartment door was open.

"Max is waiting for you," Mama said. She never said hello when Rosie came home. But she did give her a quick kiss on the cheek. "He has spelling today."

Spelling was Max's worst subject. Maybe he would

7

have been better at spelling Yiddish. But English? Never. She had to go over and over the words with him. And half the time he wasn't even paying attention.

"Max has already been to the bakery to pick up the challah," said Mama. "Here's the ticket for tomorrow. For you to pick up the meat and vegetable stew for lunch."

I just walked in and already there is this to do and that to do, Rosie thought. But she didn't say anything out loud to Mama.

While Mama made the noodles for the Sabbath dinner, Rosie sat with Max at the kitchen table. They went over each word on his spelling list. There were a lot of *oo* words this time. *Cook. Look. Brook.*

"What's a brook?" Max asked, drawing out the strange English word.

Rosie didn't know.

"Mama, what's a brook?"

Mama turned around from the stove. Even though she was from the old country, she knew English. Better than Papa, but not as well as Freyda.

"Brook," Mama said slowly. "I haven't seen one since I left Russia." She smiled sadly. "We had a brook, a little stream, that ran behind our village. We'd walk on the rocks in the brook. In the spring, the water ran fast and tickled our bare feet." Mama laughed out loud, remembering. "No, I haven't seen a brook in

America, not here on the East Side. But there must be one somewhere." She went back to her cooking.

As soon as Mama's back was turned Max started wiggling in his seat.

"You won't learn the words that way," Rosie whispered. "Now pay attention or we'll never get done."

"Can't you just tell Mama I know the words?" Max pleaded. "Everyone's waiting for me downstairs—Natie, Moey, Solly. I have a sugar cube for Bony. They want to hear him whinny for me."

"Soon," Rosie said. "It's not time for the horses to be brought to the stable yet, anyway. And it wouldn't do any good to lie to Mama. Do you want to get slapped again with the teacher's ruler for not knowing your spelling?"

Max stopped wiggling and went on with his spelling.

When he finally knew the words, Rosie let him go. He jumped up so fast, he knocked the chair over and made Mama turn.

"Oy. Where is that boy running?" said Mama. "I was going to ask him to buy more potatoes. Here. You go for me, Rosie. And quickly. The Sabbath will start soon."

Rosie took the coins from Mama, glad for the chance to get outside again.

The hustle, bustle, and noise of the street was even greater than usual, as people rushed about getting ready for the Sabbath. Rosie bought the potatoes from the

first vegetable cart she saw, and slowly walked back up the street.

The wagons were coming back to the stable now. There was old Bony, standing outside, still hitched up. And there were Max, Natie, Moey, and Solly, patting the horse's bony black sides.

Rosie felt sorry for Bony. His owner skimped on his feed and Bony was always hungry. No wonder he would whinny when he saw Max coming with those sugar cubes. Funny, Mama never noticed all those missing sugar cubes.

Rosie stopped to pat Bony, but she wouldn't let him near the potatoes. She listened to the boys making plans to go to the river the next day after services in the synagogue. They could stand there for hours and watch the tugboats and ferries going to and from Brooklyn. Rosie knew this from the hours she had spent with Max by the river when he was little and it was her job to watch him. But now he was six years old and could go without her.

"Be careful," Rosie warned Max. "You don't want to come home with another broken head. Like the last time."

"Those Clinton Streeters!" Max said angrily. "They started up with us first. Trying to kick us out of our own clubhouse like that."

Rosie had seen the "clubhouse." A pile of old wood held together by a few nails in a junk-filled lot. But to her brother and his friends, it was paradise. And they defended it from all the other gangs, much to Mama's horror.

"Well, stay clear of Clinton Street," Rosie said. "Especially on the Sabbath. Mama doesn't need any more trouble."

When Rosie got home, she had to peel the carrots. Mama diced the carrots and mixed them with potatoes, onions, sugar, and meaty bones for a carrot *tsimmes*.

Just then Freyda burst into the kitchen, her feather boa wrapped around her neck. The smell of sweet lilac perfume floated ahead of her. She bent down and gave Rosie a kiss.

"Where's Max?" Freyda said. "Doesn't he have homework?"

"We finished a little early," Rosie explained. "He's outside with Bony."

"You're so good with him," Freyda said to Rosie. "You should be a teacher."

Rosie cringed. Awful Miss Callahan popped into her thoughts. She certainly did not want to grow up and be like Miss Callahan. She'd much rather be like Freyda. Bouncy and bright and pretty.

Freyda kissed Mama on the cheek.

"You're beautiful," she said.

"Pooh, pooh," answered Mama. "Enough with the beautiful this and that. You want me to forget that you're working tomorrow, on the Sabbath."

"No, Mama, I mean it. Anyway, I know nothing will make you forget that. At least I'm home early to help you now. And I mean it about Rosie, too."

"I don't want to be a teacher," said Rosie. "I want to be like you, Freyda. All dressed up. Joking and laughing with—"

"Do you think we laugh all day long?" her sister interrupted. "While we bend over the sewing machines in that crowded room, stitching sleeve after sleeve onto a shirtwaist? Stay in school till you're older, Rosie. Be smart!"

Rosie made a face. Freyda just doesn't understand, she thought. I'm old enough now.

Sabbath Dinner

By the time Papa came home, his clothes all splattered with paint, the kitchen was shining. The table was set with the Sabbath cloth and dishes.

Mama had already lit the candles, waving her hands above them in circles to bring the light and warmth toward her.

It was hard work getting ready for the Sabbath, Rosie thought. But it was worth it. All the rest of the week it was so busy. But on Fridays everyone came home early. Everyone washed and put on clean clothes. And everyone sat together.

Even Freyda. No union meeting. No movie or date to see a friend tonight. She was right there next to Rosie. Just like she used to be. Max sat across the table in between Mama and Papa, so they could watch him.

Papa sang the blessings over the wine and bread. Then Mama brought out the bowls of rich chicken soup bubbling with fat and little specks of green and orange, celery and carrots.

While everyone ate the chicken, noodles, and carrot *tsimmes*, Mama and Papa talked. About the stories in the *Forward*, the Yiddish newspaper. About their neighbors and friends.

"Have you seen Mrs. Feingult's new boarder yet?" Mama asked Papa.

"A good man from the old country," Papa said, and winked at Freyda. "A friend of her cousin's."

"He can't speak a word of English," said Freyda.

Papa sighed.

"What are we going to do with her?" he asked Mama, giving a nod toward Freyda. "Our modern American daughter. The old ways, the old language are no good anymore."

"I didn't say that," Freyda argued.

"No. But I see it," said Papa. "All the old ways going. Out the window. Poof. Just like that."

"Oh, Papa." Freyda sighed.

Papa's starting again, Rosie thought. She knew what he would say next.

"I never thought a daughter of mine would work on the Sabbath," he said.

Mama nodded in agreement. "What can we do?" she whispered.

Papa shrugged his shoulders.

Freyda looked at her hands. Max hummed.

"And all the time she wastes with those union meetings!" Papa shook his head.

"It's not a waste," said Freyda, unable to be quiet any longer. "If you only knew how bad the factory conditions are. How dirty. How unsafe. How—"

"I know. I know," said Papa. "But if you remembered how bad things were in Russia, you would appreciate what you have here. At least here we are not killed for no reason. A Jew in Russia never knows when a riot will start, a beating, a fire."

"Does that make it right, what they do here?" Freyda answered. "Locking us in so we can't cheat them of a minute of work time? Timing our trips to the bathroom? Bad lighting? Crowded workrooms, long hours, poor pay? One little fire escape for a big factory building and no sprinkler system?"

For once, Papa didn't answer. Max wiggled.

"Well, I'm going to bed," said Freyda. She stood up and pushed her chair back. She nodded in Rosie's direction.

Rosie glanced at her parents and looked down. Why does Freyda always put me in the middle? she thought.

"I'm coming," she mumbled to her sister. But first she helped Mama clear the table.

By the time Rosie crept into the bed she shared with Freyda in the tiny back room, her sister was already asleep.

Clanging Bells

The next morning, Freyda woke Rosie up.

"I have to go to work soon," she said. She leaned over Rosie, who was still snuggled under the blanket. "Do you want me to fix your hair?"

Freyda must still feel bad about last night, Rosie thought. It wasn't every day she offered to brush and put up Rosie's long brown hair.

Rosie sat up in bed, enjoying the feel of Freyda's brush. Freyda never pulled or hurt the way Mama did.

The apartment was quiet. Mama, Papa, and Max

were still sleeping in the front room. Mama kept their mattresses hidden behind the door during the day. Saturday, the Sabbath, was the only day they slept past six A.M. The only day the shouts of the peddlers and butchers and delivery-wagon drivers didn't fill the streets.

Then Rosie heard someone coming up the stairs.

"It's Celia," said Freyda. "I'll have to finish."

The footsteps were light, quick. Celia was in a hurry.

She burst into the apartment without knocking and ran into the bedroom. No one ever knocked on the East Side.

"Harry gave me a ring!" Tiny, pretty Celia was almost dancing, her face all flushed and beaming with her good news. "I'm engaged!"

Freyda jumped up and hugged her cousin. She was so happy for her. "Finally, Harry asked you! It must be because he got that job in the hat shop."

Celia nodded. She could hardly talk, she was so full of her good news.

"How can someone sleep? Such noise!" Mama came into the little room. Celia waved her hand with the engagement ring toward Mama.

"Oy, my little Celia! A bride already!"

"Aunt Yetta, I'm almost seventeen!" Celia argued. But Rosie could tell she loved being the center of attention for once.

"Uh-oh. We have to hurry," said Freyda. "It's late."

"Show Papa your ring," Mama told Celia. "On your way out."

Celia and Freyda left for the factory. Soon Mama, Papa, Max, and Rosie would go to Sabbath services in their little neighborhood synagogue.

"Don't forget to pick up the stew for lunch after services," Mama told Rosie. "Don't forget the ticket."

Even on the Sabbath I have to do this and that, Rosie thought. But she didn't say anything. Instead she felt inside her pocket for the piece of paper. The one that said, "Changes ahead." That made her feel better.

After services, Max and his friends escaped to the river. Rosie had to go to the bakery. Sarah went with her. Rosie didn't like to go alone, although Sarah wasn't much help. She was even more scared than Rosie.

Down the wooden steps into the cellar of the bakery they went. The apartments where they lived didn't have ovens. So almost everyone in the neighborhood brought their breads and stews and cakes here to be baked.

Rosie liked the bakers, big men dressed in white. Their hair and arms and faces were dusted white with flour. Rosie always felt as if she were going into another world when she went down to the ovens. And she liked watching the men put the cakes and stews into and out of the enormous ovens with their big wooden paddles.

What she didn't like were the gray rats that darted about the cellar floor. The bakers didn't seem to mind them, but Rosie did. She stepped down carefully and gave a baker her ticket.

"Mrs. Friedman's stew pot," she said. She tried not to cry out as each rat scurried past her.

Sarah never even left the stairs.

The iron pot was heavy, filled with meat and beans and vegetables, but Rosie practically flew up the steps with it. Sarah raced ahead of her. They both sighed with relief when they reached the street. They took turns carrying the pot home.

After lunch, Rosie walked down to Sarah's building. She missed all the weekday activity of her street. It was calm and almost empty. Everywhere the stores were closed, the pushcarts gone, the horses resting for the day in the stables near Delancey Street.

But the whole afternoon stretched before her. No school, no helping Max with homework.

She and Sarah sat on the wooden cellar door in front of Sarah's building. They talked about mean Miss Callahan and Izzie and the other kids in their school. They played house and store by themselves, and tag and prisoner's base with Anna and Louis, who lived in the building. The afternoon hours sped by quickly and peacefully. Then suddenly the sounds of fire engine bells startled them.

They all stopped what they were doing and ran toward the sound of the clanging bells. As they turned the corner, three large white horses pulling a red fire wagon with hoses thundered past them. Followed by another. And another one loaded with ladders.

"Must be a big fire," said Sarah.

Clang clang. They heard even more fire bells on other streets. There were a lot of fires on the East Side. But so many wagons . . .

People were running down the street after the wagons. Rosie and Sarah stopped an old woman with a kerchief on her head, still wearing her apron.

"Have you heard?" Rosie asked her. "Where's the fire?"

"Washington Square," the woman answered.

They looked up over the buildings toward the square. In the distance, a pillar of black smoke rose into the sky.

"Freyda works there," Rosie said quietly.

"I know," said Sarah.

The Fire

Mama and Papa were busy when Rosie burst through the door. Busy with Max.

As soon as Rosie looked at him, she knew what had happened. A street fight. He was muddy all over and his shirt was ripped. He had scratches on his face and a puffy eye.

Mama looked up. "Such a nice shirt," she said. "Feh. And the socks. All torn." She shook her head.

"I told you not to go down Clinton Street," said Rosie, pointing her finger at Max.

"Didn't need to," said Max. "They were over by the river."

"Oh," said Rosie. Then she remembered Sarah waiting downstairs and the fire engines and the old woman in the kerchief.

"Mama, I'm going to see a fire with Sarah."

"I'm going, too," said Max.

"You stay right here," said Mama, pointing to the chair.

Luckily, Mama didn't ask any questions. Rosie didn't want to say more. Mama didn't need other worries.

Rosie left the apartment so fast, she almost tumbled down the old stairs.

"What took you so long?" asked Sarah. "I was about to come up and get you."

"It was just Max. He got into trouble again. Let's go."

Up Eldridge Street and down Houston Street, they ran. Other people were running, too. The air was still filled with the sound of clanging bells.

Soon they left their neighborhood, the Jewish neighborhood, and ran through the streets where the Italians lived. Here the stores weren't closed for the Jewish Sabbath. The streets were filled with people and peddlers and activity.

They passed a scissors grinder turning the wheel that

made his grindstone go. Two boys squatted on the sidewalk rubbing their customers' shoes back and forth, back and forth with a cloth, giving them a shine. Rosie could smell the big hot pretzels lined up on spokes coming out of an old lady's basket. She and Sarah ran on. To Washington Square. Faster and faster.

More and more people were running. Soon they were part of a large crowd, everyone trying to find the fire, to find their daughters, husbands, sisters, cousins. Fires were serious business on the East Side. Scary business.

Now they were on Greene Street, running around people to get closer to Freyda's building, the Asch Building. Freyda worked on one of the top floors, making shirtwaists. So did Celia.

The policemen, all red-faced and serious, were trying to set up ropes to keep the crowd from coming too close to the fire.

Galloping horses pulling the fire engines and ambulances raced up to the crowd. Only then did the crowd move aside.

There were people on all sides of Rosie now. Pushing. Shouting. Weeping. Screaming.

Rosie was used to crowds. Crowds on the busy market streets. Crowds gathered around an accident, a funeral, a wedding couple, a fight.

But Rosie had never been in such a big crowd before.

She grabbed for Sarah's hand and found it. Sarah was shaking. Was it from the running? Rosie wondered. Or . . .

Rosie looked around her. People everywhere. She couldn't see past the people. Who could she ask? She was almost too afraid to ask. What if someone said the terrible words and named Freyda's building? But she had to know. So she reached up and tapped the shoulder of a heavy woman in a purple shawl standing in front of her.

The woman turned.

"The building," Rosie asked. "Which building is it?"

"The Asch Building," the woman answered. "The top three floors." She shook her head sadly. "The firemen's ladders only reach the sixth floor."

Rosie gasped. The words sent shudders through her body.

"Sarah. Did you hear that, Sarah?"

Sarah just nodded, stunned.

"I've got to get closer," said Rosie. "And see for myself."

"But how can we do that?" Sarah argued. "Look at all these people."

"We've got to," said Rosie. She pulled Sarah along behind her through the crowd, not daring to let go of her hand.

As they got closer to the building Rosie looked up.

She could see the firemen in their black coats and black hats on high water towers. They were pouring steady streams of water on the big gray building.

One, two, three, four, five . . . Counting the streams of water helped. Six, seven, eight, nine, ten.

Rosie couldn't see the ground by the building. There were too many people in front of her, beside her, all around her. And she couldn't get any closer. There was crying, shouting, pushing. She felt like she was part of a giant monster. Sometimes the wind carried some of the spray from the hoses over the monster.

Suddenly, the crowd broke near Rosie. A woman struggled through, going the wrong way, away from the building. Her long hair had come loose and her clothing was torn and smoke-smudged.

The sight of the woman woke Rosie up as if from a bad dream.

"Ida. That's Ida, Freyda's friend," she yelled at Sarah. "Let's catch up to her. Maybe she knows what happened to the others."

Rosie and Sarah followed Ida. Still holding hands, they made their way back through the crowd.

Ida reached for the woman in the purple shawl, the nice one who had talked to Rosie.

"I've got to get home," Ida cried. "Take me home."

"There, there," said the woman in a soft voice. "Of course I'll take you home."

Rosie couldn't wait any longer. "Ida!" she shouted.

She pulled on Ida's skirt, trying to get her attention. "Have you seen Freyda? Celia? Have you, Ida?"

But Ida just stared blankly ahead of her and didn't say a word.

"Do you know where she lives?" asked the woman.

"Yes. She lives near me on Rivington Street."

"Take us there," said the woman. "She's in shock. See how pale she is? How quickly she breathes? We've got to get her home."

"But . . . but . . . ," Rosie stuttered. She didn't want to leave the fire. She had to stay. To find Freyda. And Celia.

Sarah squeezed Rosie's hand. "I have to go, too. It's late. My mama will worry."

So Rosie and Sarah led Ida and the woman in the purple shawl through the crowd, away from the fire.

"I'm coming back," Rosie muttered to herself. "I'll get Papa and come back."

Everything
Burning

It wasn't until they were near Rivington Street that Ida started talking. It was as if the sight of her street woke up something inside her.

"Everything burning," she said. Her breathing was fast and loud.

The woman patted Ida on the shoulder. Her name was Bessie, Rosie had learned on the trip home.

"Don't talk. Save your energy," Bessie said firmly.

But Rosie wanted Ida to talk. Maybe then she would say something about Freyda. About Celia.

"Smoke. . . . Choked. . . . "

Now that Ida had started, it seemed like she couldn't be quiet. The more she talked, the more sense she made, until she was finally speaking in full sentences.

"I was right next to the elevator. First it went past us. We yelled and screamed. When it finally stopped and the door opened, I was catching fire." She touched the edge of her dress. Rosie could see where part of it was scorched and brown.

"The elevator car filled up so fast. I jumped in on top of the other girls. The door was closing. Someone grabbed my hair and tried to pull me out. I kicked them." Ida sighed. "I almost didn't . . ." Her voice trailed off and then picked up again.

"When we got to the bottom, the firemen wouldn't let us out of the building. They were afraid that the bodies falling out of the windows would hurt us." Here Ida stopped and shuddered.

"I stood there. Screaming. Then two men helped me across the street into a store."

Ida stopped. She looked around her. For the first time, she really saw Rosie and Sarah and the strange lady whose arm was still on her shoulder.

"I'm just helping," Bessie answered when Ida stared at her.

Something clicked inside Ida's head. She turned to Rosie. "Freyda. Is she all right?"

"What?" Rosie's face crumbled in disappointment.

"I was hoping you'd seen her and you could tell me."

"She was on the floor above me, the ninth," Ida said simply. "I don't know."

"Celia?"

"I don't know."

Ida was quiet again. Her shoulders started shaking.

"Let's get her home," Bessie said. "Fast."

Ida's building was close to the corner. Luckily she didn't live on the top floor. They knocked on her door. Her father, a small, neatly dressed man with a full beard, answered the door.

"So, *nu?* This is the way my daughter comes home?" he said when he saw Ida. His face looked angry.

Ida drew back.

Bessie looked puzzled.

"He's very strict. She's afraid of him," Rosie whispered.

Bessie held on to Ida's shoulder. "She must lie down, sir," Bessie said politely. "There's been a fire. Let me explain."

Bessie went into the dark apartment with Ida. Rosie, eager to get back to the fire, ran down the stairs with Sarah. They said good-bye at the door.

"Tell me as soon as you know anything," said Sarah.

"I will," said Rosie.

As she hurried down the street to her own building, her mind was a jumble. She pushed open the door. The smell of the hallway, the feel of the smooth banister under her hand were all a comfort. She breathed in deeply as she reached the top of the stairs.

Fire. Bodies. Smoke. Ladders. Hoses. Ambulances. Ida. Pushing. Shoving. Screaming. What would she tell Mama first?

But all her thoughts fled when she heard the water running, the crying and screaming coming from her own apartment.

Maybe Mama already knows, she thought.

Rosie burst into the front room, where the voices were coming from. There was Freyda standing by the table, Papa next to her. Her clothes were all torn and soiled, her beautiful new velvet hat and her boa gone. The perfume smell was gone, too. Instead there was the smell of fire and burnt flesh, smoke and sweat. Her face was stained with tears and black with soot, her arm red with a burn. But it was Freyda. Really Freyda. Alive!

Rosie rushed up to hug her sister.

"I couldn't find you," Rosie sobbed with relief. "I was so worried."

"I got out. Thank God," Freyda said in a strange, flat voice, not at all like her usual dancing one. "Not everyone was as lucky as me." She stared ahead blankly, reminding Rosie suddenly of Ida.

Mama came running in from the kitchen. "Freyda shouldn't talk," she said as she wiped Freyda's face

with a wet cloth. "She just got home. And where were you?"

"At the fire. I told you when you were taking care of Max," Rosie said. Mama seemed to have forgotten in all the confusion. "We brought Ida home," Rosie added.

"Thank God," muttered Mama. "Another one safe."

Max came in carrying a blanket. He was all cleaned up.

Papa helped Freyda to the couch so she could lie down. She fell asleep immediately.

"Do you think we should get the doctor?" said Papa.

"Yes," said Mama. "And I'll make us all a cup of hot tea. Very hot."

One More Question

Freyda slept all that night and the next morning, too. The doctor had said to let her sleep as long as she needed.

She couldn't go to work that day anyway, thought Rosie. There was no factory left. She shuddered.

Rosie was in the front room when Freyda woke up in the afternoon. At first, she still seemed dazed. She looked about her as if wondering why she was on the couch. Why she was sleeping in the middle of the day. Why she wasn't at work.

Then she started sobbing.

She remembers, thought Rosie.

Mama and Papa heard her and came. So did Max.

Freyda sat up. "The flames," she began. "Trapped. We were trapped." The words tumbled out as if Freyda could not stop them.

Mama patted her. "Lie down, Freyda. Rest."

But Freyda went on talking and sobbing, telling her story.

"I was in the coatroom when it started. Celia, too. They had just paid us. I remember putting the money into the top of my stocking."

Freyda bent down and touched her leg.

"Don't worry," Mama said. "It was still there."

Freyda sighed. She went on. "It wasn't safe in the coatroom. The walls were smoking. It wasn't safe in the shop, either. Girls were all over the floor. They had fainted. People stepped on them. Girls were trying to climb onto the sewing machine tables. Some ran with their hair burning. There was pushing, shoving, screaming."

Mama gasped at Freyda's words. She had to sit down, too.

"I looked for Celia," Freyda continued. "She had been right next to me. But she was gone. Oh, Celia." Freyda's sobs filled the room.

"It was so hot in the stairway." She talked quickly

now, as if she had to get her whole story out as fast as she could.

"I ran back into the shop and found a roll of some material. I think it was lawn. You know, that sheer kind of cotton. I wrapped myself in it, around and around until I was completely covered except for my face.

"I ran back into the stairway and the fire. Up, up. I couldn't breathe.

"The material caught fire. I kept running, twisting and turning at the same time, so the burning fabric would peel off behind me.

"The next floor, the tenth, was empty. Only the sound of the fire burning, burning. I didn't know that one more flight of stairs and I would be on the roof. I didn't know.

"I heard someone call, 'Come to the roof! Come to the roof!'

"I saw Mr. Gordon, the bookkeeper, in the stairway. He was holding a stack of record books. He was nodding toward the stairs.

"I ran after him. The stairway was even hotter than before. By the time I got to the roof, most of that material was in ashes on the staircase. A little piece of it was still under my arm." Here Freyda pointed to her burn.

"But I was on the roof. There we were, many of us.

Coughing. Screaming. Burning. Safe." Freyda sighed.

"The students from next door helped us over the roofs and down to the street. But what I saw there made me run away. Run home. Bodies. Bodies falling from the windows like so many bolts of cloth. Bodies on the sidewalk."

No one said a word.

Finally, Rosie asked the question for all of them.

"Was one of them Celia?"

Freyda shook her head. "I didn't look," she said. "I couldn't. I ran away. Home." Freyda stared straight ahead. No one asked any more questions.

Changes Ahead

They found out about Celia when Uncle George, Celia's father, came with the news.

They knew it wasn't good news as soon as they saw his face.

He sat at the table, head down, playing with the sugar cube Mama had offered him for his tea.

"It was her ring," he said simply. "That's how we knew it was her. By her ring."

Mama nodded, tears falling down her face.

Papa sat quietly, his arm around Freyda.

Max took a sugar cube and put it in his pocket. No one noticed except Rosie. She also saw the tears in his eyes. She looked down at the table.

In her mind, Rosie pictured that morning just two days before when Celia had bounced up the steps and showed them her new ring, the one Harry had given her. It seemed so long ago. When Celia was alive.

"If only she had listened to me," said Uncle George. "If only she hadn't gone to work on the Sabbath."

Everyone was quiet. Rosie waited for Freyda to say something. But she didn't.

Rosie couldn't stand the silence. "That's not it," she blurted out. "It could have been a Sunday. Or a Monday. A Tuesday. Next month. Next year."

Suddenly Rosie saw that everyone was staring at her. "Didn't you hear Freyda? Ida? Yussel down the hall? The doors were locked. The windows stuck. Scraps all over the floor. Oil-soaked scraps. Hundreds of sewing machines packed into one room. Fires in the stairway. Only one fire escape. And it didn't even reach the ground." Rosie stopped.

"Sorry," she said. She got up to leave the room.

"No. Stay here." It was Papa. "Rosie is right. So is Freyda," he said unexpectedly. "This isn't Russia. It is America. But people burn here, too. Unless we say something. Do something."

"Then I can go Wednesday, Papa?" asked Freyda. "To the meeting?"

Rosie noticed that for the first time since the fire, Freyda's voice had a little of the dance to it.

Papa nodded.

Mama looked at him, puzzled.

"The unions," he said in answer to her unspoken question. "Maybe a good thing."

"Maybe," Mama agreed.

"I want to go, too," Rosie said. "I'm old enough now."

Mama and Papa looked at Freyda. "If Freyda wants," said Mama.

Freyda reached for her sister's hand. "It's a meeting to honor the memory of those who died in the fire. You can go if you want to," she said.

The meeting was at night in the Grand Central Palace.

The crowd was as big as the one at the fire, Rosie thought. But the fire was over. And 146 people had died.

The crowd was a sad one, an angry one, a tense one. But they didn't push and shove like the one on Greene Street. They know now, Rosie thought. Who lived through the fire. And who didn't.

Rosie noticed all the policemen standing around the huge hall. Waiting. For what? Rosie wondered. She reached for Freyda's hand. Were they expecting trouble?

A union was sponsoring the meeting. Freyda explained what the letters ILGWU meant. They stood for International Ladies' Garment Workers' Union.

"ILGWU is easier," said Rosie.

"It's the union I'm in," said Freyda. "Ladies' garments. Shirtwaists. But all the unions do the same thing. They try to get better working conditions, better pay, and shorter days for factory workers."

She stopped talking. The speakers had begun.

It was hard for Rosie to understand the speeches. And people were shouting at the speakers, booing and hissing them.

They're angry about the fire, she thought. Angry and sad.

Suddenly, everyone quieted down. Freyda bent down and whispered in Rosie's ear. "A moment of silent prayer for the dead," she said.

Just low murmurs filled the hall now. Until someone sobbed. The sob pulled at Rosie, tugged at the raw place where she missed Celia. At the place that was sore from seeing all the funeral carriages moving through the crowded East Side streets. From seeing all the flowers fixed on the doors.

Rosie remembered the fear, the shivers, as she had stood on Greene Street behind Bessie, the woman in the purple shawl.

She was part of that monster again. The pushing, shoving, screaming monster. She was caught. She couldn't move. People were sobbing all around her now. And calling out names. The sound of names echoed through the hall. Now they knew the names. Now they knew.

Rosalie.

Lucia.

Abe.

Esther.

Sophie.

Della.

Italian names.

Jewish names.

Men's names.

Women's names.

Mostly women's names.

Someone fainted near Rosie. A policeman struggled through the crowd to help her. The monster moved to make room for him. Alarms sounded. Doctors. Ambulances.

The names went on.

Bettina.

Sara.

Celia.

It was Freyda who sobbed out Celia's name. Freyda, who was there next to her.

There were no more names. The monster disappeared. Rosie was in a crowd once again listening tospeakers. This time, she could hear what the man was saying.

"Your future lies in unions. If you organize yourselves, you gain strength and get better working conditions. There must not be another fire like the Triangle Shirtwaist Company fire."

Rosie pulled on Freyda's sleeve. "That's what you were trying to do," she whispered into her ear. "Wasn't it?"

"Yes," said Freyda. "It is. That's what the strike was about last year. Remember? We didn't go to work for thirteen weeks. And I stood outside the factory with signs like, GIVE US A 52-HOUR WORK WEEK. There was even a sign that said, WE NEED MORE FIRE ESCAPES. I have a feeling there'll be a lot more people to help us now."

"I want to help," said Rosie.

"But Rosie, you know what I think. I haven't changed my mind about you and school. If anything—"

"No. That's not what I mean, Freyda. I'll stay in school. But I want to work for the union, too. I can help. I can give out leaflets. Go with you to meetings. We could do some things together, like we used to. Can I?"

Freyda smiled. A real smile.

"Like we used to," she agreed. "When I was younger and we were both in school. But we'll have to ask Mama and Papa." She grew thoughtful for a minute. "I have a feeling Papa will say yes. Don't you?"

"And Mama, too," Rosie said, thinking how things had changed since the fire. How Mama and Papa and Freyda and she had changed.

Then, with some excitement, she thought of the fortune-teller's piece of paper. She felt around in her pocket to see if it was still there. It was. Rosie pulled it out.

"Changes ahead," she whispered out loud.

"What's that?" Freyda asked.

"Oh, just a silly fortune Sarah and I got from the old lady and her parrot," Rosie said. "Don't tell Mama," she added as she tucked the paper back in her pocket.

Yes, there would be some changes ahead, Rosie was sure. Changes for her and for Freyda, for the unions and the factory workers.

They weren't the changes she had thought about less than a week before, when they had spent Sarah's penny. But maybe, just maybe, they'd be better.

ABOUT THIS BOOK

Shirtwaists were a popular item of women's clothing in 1911. They buttoned down the front and had a collar like a man's shirt, but were made of a sheer cotton fabric that tapered to a fitted waistline and so were considered attractive and feminine.

Shirtwaists and other garments were sewn in sweatshops, often by immigrants who worked long hours for little pay. Conditions were poor in these factories and safety precautions minimal.

Out of about 500 workers, 146 died when one of these sweatshops, the Triangle Shirtwaist Company, burst into flame on March 25, 1911. The tragedy of the fire shocked the people of New York City in a way nothing else had, and brought to their attention the need for factory reform.

Citywide protests were held. Relief funds were set up for the families of victims of the fire. Some money was even sent to families in Europe who depended on checks from their relatives in America.

A Bureau of Fire Prevention was established and the

powers and duties of the Fire Commissioner were en-
larged. Labor unions, which represented the factory
workers, grew in numbers and in strength.

The Asch Building, site of the Triangle Shirtwaist
Company fire, still stands at the corner of Greene
Street and Washington Place. Inside there are offices.
But the plaque on the front reminds us that this is
where 146 factory workers died.

To help me write the story of Rosie and her family,
I walked through the streets of the section of New
York City now called the Lower East Side. This is
where they would have lived and where the fire actually
took place. I read newspaper accounts of the fire—
"how the fire started, no one knows" (*The New York
Times*)—and memoirs by people who lived at the time.
And I visited the New York City Fire Museum, which
has photos of the fire and actual fire trucks used in 1911.

While working on this book, I often thought of my
grandfather Joe. He was a presser of ladies' cloaks and
suits, and worked in the garment industry at the time
of the Triangle fire. My mother remembers him taking
her one day to see the Asch Building and saying to
her, "Hanna, that is where the big fire was."

He would tell her that some bosses were good. Some
were not. Sometimes there was work. Sometimes there
wasn't. But he always paid his union dues because he
believed that unions made things better for the workers.

B.D.G.